THE MAGICAL UNICORN SOCIETY

THE GOLDEN UNICORN

SECRETS & LEGENDS

Michael O'Mara Books Limited

With special thanks to Adrian Bott,
Jonny Leighton and Anne Marie Ryan

Edited by Jonny Leighton
Designed by Jack Clucas
Cover design by Angie Allison

Illustrations by Aitch, Oana Befort and Rae Ritchie
Front cover illustration by Harry and Zanna Goldhawk
Back cover illustration by Aitch

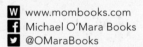

First published in Great Britain in 2019 by Michael O'Mara Books
Limited, 9 Lion Yard, Tremadoc Road, London SW4 7NQ

W www.mombooks.com
f Michael O'Mara Books
@OMaraBooks

A CIP catalogue record for this book is available from the British Library.

ISBN: 978-1-78929-155-1

2 4 6 8 10 9 7 5 3 1

Printed in China

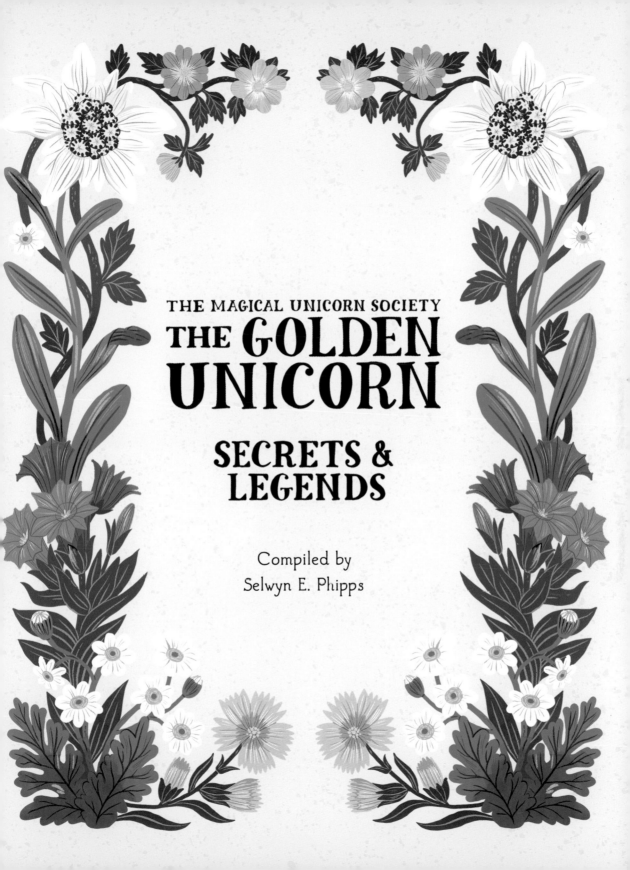

THE MAGICAL UNICORN SOCIETY

THE GOLDEN UNICORN

SECRETS & LEGENDS

Compiled by
Selwyn E. Phipps

CONTENTS

Est. 1577

WELCOME

Greetings, unicorn lovers.

My name is Selwyn E. Phipps, the current president of the Magical Unicorn Society. The Society unites people across the globe who love unicorns. It has branches in many countries and has existed for hundreds of years. We are always learning more about unicorns and the adventurers, explorers and ordinary folk who have encountered these extraordinary creatures.

I'm delighted to introduce *The Golden Unicorn: Secrets and Legends* – a collection of eight very special, never-before-told unicorn sightings to share with you. I gathered the details contained in each case study from the archives of our London headquarters – from ancient diaries, typed reports, newspaper

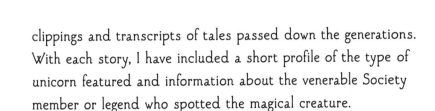

clippings and transcripts of tales passed down the generations.
With each story, I have included a short profile of the type of
unicorn featured and information about the venerable Society
member or legend who spotted the magical creature.

This book is a tribute to the work of many M.U.S. members.
Whenever we think there's nothing more to discover, someone's
intrepid exploration turns up new and exciting information to
surprise and delight us. For instance, we once thought that there
were only seven unicorn families, but last year an eighth family,
the Dawn Spirits, was discovered. This closely guarded secret
is described in this book, for the first time.

Anyone can come across a unicorn – it's often just a case of
keeping your eyes peeled and your ears alert. Why not become
a member of our Society? Find out details of how to join at the
back of this book.

I hope you enjoy these very special unicorn tales. I'm so excited
to be sharing them with you!

Selwyn

101st PRESIDENT OF THE
MAGICAL UNICORN SOCIETY

For secrets and legends throughout the ages,

Settle back and turn these pages ...

The Golden Unicorn

The Golden Unicorn was one of the first unicorns to spring into existence, back when the world was bursting with magic.

Horn made of solid gold

Delicate strands of golden hair

This unicorn sparkles with magic and has the power of invisibility

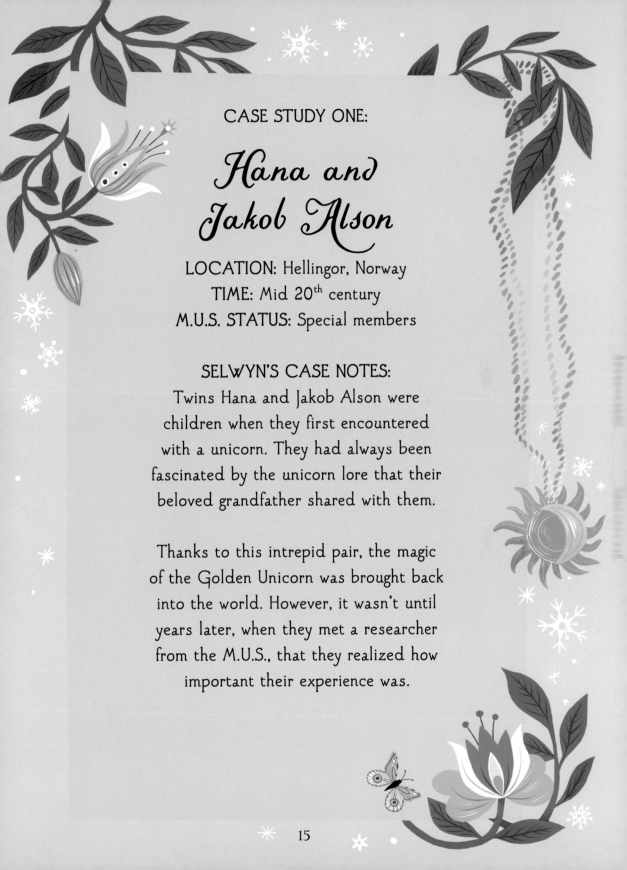

CASE STUDY ONE:

Hana and Jakob Alson

LOCATION: Hellingor, Norway
TIME: Mid 20th century
M.U.S. STATUS: Special members

SELWYN'S CASE NOTES:

Twins Hana and Jakob Alson were children when they first encountered with a unicorn. They had always been fascinated by the unicorn lore that their beloved grandfather shared with them.

Thanks to this intrepid pair, the magic of the Golden Unicorn was brought back into the world. However, it wasn't until years later, when they met a researcher from the M.U.S., that they realized how important their experience was.

The Golden
Unicorn Returns

Nestled snugly between towering Norwegian mountains covered in thick forest, there was a small town called Hellingor, where it had been winter for a hundred years. The cobbled streets were coated in glittering frost and the river, coiled around the town like a silver snake, was frozen solid.

The people who lived there wore the thickest of coats all year round and were often found huddled indoors beside crackling fires, drinking hot, spiced drinks to keep them warm.

No one knew what had happened to plunge the area into an endless winter, but more than one person suspected magic. It had been Midsummer's Eve when the chill descended. The first snows had glowed gold and silver and the wind howled with a strange energy. Nothing natural could have made this sudden winter last so long.

"I bet it was witches," said Hana, confidently. "Didn't they live in the hills above the town?"

"Witches?" Jakob laughed. "You've been reading too many fairy tales."

"No I haven't," Hana insisted. "You know Grandad always said there was magic in this place. If *you're* so clever, what do *you* think happened?"

Jakob wasn't sure. For the children of Hellingor the frost, ice and snow was so normal they didn't remember anything else. Green grass and hot summers were something they'd only read about in old books.

"Unicorns?" Jakob suggested, with a shrug. Unicorns were another of the local legends that their grandfather loved. He used to tell stories about the different types that roamed the world and how they each had their own magic powers.

"Do you mean the story about the Golden Unicorn and the Dragon?" Hana asked. "It could be that. Or it could be that Hellingor is just cursed with terrible weather!"

The twins laughed and hurried on, making their way out of the town and through the woods. They were headed towards the hills, dragging their sledge behind them. School was out, so they were going to make the most of the fresh snow. They could worry about why it was forever winter another time.

After a minute or two, Jakob grabbed Hana and pointed towards a thick clump of pine trees.

"Quiet!" he hissed. "Through there – I think I can see one."

"One what?" Hana asked, peering into the mass of snowy branches ahead. "A unicorn? I can't see anything."

Suddenly, she felt a tingling on the back of her neck. She turned around just as Jakob shoved a handful of snow down the back of her coat.

"Hey!" she yelled, while her brother doubled over laughing.
"I knew you were going to do something like that."

"Oh yeah?" he replied. "As if you weren't going to do the same
thing when my back was turned!"

Hana and Jakob were always playing jokes on each other. Yet,
strangely, it was hard to catch each other out. Their grandfather
said it was something to do with being twins. They had a special
bond between them.

When they were tiny, their grandfather had given them
nicknames: Jakob was the sun and Hana was the moon. He said
it was because they were the two most important things in the
sky and that, just like the twins, they were magically linked.
Before he died, he made little sun and moon pendants. Hana
and Jakob treasured them, and wore them every day.

The twins emerged from the woods and began the steep climb
up the slope. Jakob put on a burst of speed.

"Last one there's an ugly old witch," he called. Hana had
no choice but to follow – she couldn't let her brother win.

Jakob raced to the top of the ridge, dragging the sledge behind him. But when he stopped to catch his breath, he couldn't see Hana anywhere. Frowning, he scanned the hillside.

"Hana?" he called, his voice echoing around the silent valley. "Hana! Stop messing around." But there was no reply. He wondered if *she* was playing a trick on *him*, when he felt a strange, tingling sensation around his neck. He rummaged inside his coat and felt for his pendant. He felt the little sun becoming warmer and pulse gently beneath his fingers. He gave a gasp of surprise – it had never done that before.

Jakob took a step back down the hill, towards where he had last seen Hana, and the pendant pulsed harder. He took a step to the side and the pendant was still.

"Strange," he murmured. "It's like it *wants* me to go somewhere."

Sure enough, as he took careful steps down the snowy slope, his pendant pulsed steadily, guiding him like a magical compass. Jakob followed its lead until he came to a rocky cave in the side of the hill. He wondered how had he never noticed it before.

Creeping forwards, his fingers on the sun pendant around his neck, Jakob saw a familiar figure appear through the gloom of the cave – it was Hana!

"Hey," he said, more relieved than annoyed. "You could've told me you were going to wander off!"

"Sorry," she whispered. "It was just ... I felt this tugging on my necklace and I had to follow it ..."

She pulled out her moon pendant and showed Jakob – it shone with magical light and was pulsing just like his.

"Weird. It's like ... *magic*," Jakob said, frowning.

"It's not *like* magic," Hana replied, much more seriously and looking at him with wide eyes. "It *is* magic."

"So what do we do?" Jakob asked.

"We follow wherever the pendants take us," she said. "I'm beginning to think Grandad gave them to us for a reason."

Jakob nodded solemnly and together they ventured further into the cave. Icicles hung from the ceiling and the walls glistened with a rainbow of sparkling frost. They followed the beat of their pendants through frozen passages and under dripping icicles until they turned a corner and stumbled backwards in shock. Towering in front of them was a unicorn made entirely of ice.

"What *is* it?" Jakob asked, hardly believing what he saw.

The twins crept closer. The unicorn statue stood proudly, its icy gaze fixed. They peered as close as they dared and could see that deep below the layers of frost and ice, it glowed gold.

"What if this isn't just a statue?" Hana whispered. Could it be the *actual* Golden Unicorn, from Grandad's story?"

Jakob wasn't sure, but his grandfather's favourite myth about what had happened to Hellingor came back to him:

In the distant reaches of time, there lived two horses: one tawny brown and one silvery grey. They lived in a lush valley where magic shone all around. Lots of creatures made their home there, from fairies and pixies to trolls and imps. However, it was also home to the Winter Dragons, that used to terrorize the horses. The dragons would chase the horses and try to freeze them with the icy flames that burst from their mouths. Until, one day, the horses escaped the Winter Dragons by charging through a magical waterfall, that transformed them into unicorns.

The Golden and the Silver Unicorns, as they became known, then roamed the world. Whenever they bent to touch the ground with their horns, a new kind of unicorn would appear.

That is how the seven unicorn families were created.

The Golden and the Silver Unicorns, though, were incredibly elusive, and even the Magical Unicorn Society – the secretive unicorn society that the twins' grandfather often mentioned – had been unable to find them. However, the people of Hellingor knew something the M.U.S. didn't: the Golden Unicorn was the reason Hellingor was covered in ice and snow.

The two unicorns had many magical powers, but one terrible day, they became separated from one another. Alone, their powers grew weaker and they gradually lost their precious power of invisibility. A Winter Dragon spotted the Golden Unicorn and chased it to the far north, to Hellingor. Although it tried everything to evade the dragon, it had grown weak, and the dragon was able to swoop down and strike it with an icy flame.

The unicorn stumbled onwards and found shelter deep in a cave, until it finally succumbed to the dragon's wintry magic and turned to ice. In a last, desperate bid for freedom, it had sent out one final blast of magic, which had accidentally turned the area all around to ice and snow. That, according to their grandfather, was how Hellingor came to be gripped by frost and cold forevermore. And, according to him, that is how it would stay, until two people with a special bond of their own could undo the Winter Dragon's spell.

These two people would be represented by the power of the sun and the moon, just like the Golden and Silver Unicorns had been throughout history, in different cultures and kingdoms all over the world.

"Strange," Hana whispered, touching her pendant. "It's almost like we were meant to find this unicorn."

"But what are we supposed to do with it?" Jakob asked.

"We have to help it," said Hana firmly.

The twins came up with a plan. If they could get the unicorn out of the cave and into the open, maybe they could set it free of the ice? Jakob grabbed the sledge, and together they tried to drag the unicorn on to it. But they soon realized that wasn't going to work – the sledge was too small and the frozen unicorn was stuck fast.

"Stupid thing," said Jakob. "I thought it was supposed to be magic. It can't even move."

Suddenly, Hana realized something. "It *was* magic, until it became separated from the Silver Unicorn. We need some way to give it back its magic. Something that symbolizes the bond that the Golden and Silver Unicorns once had."

Jakob knew what Hana was getting at: the pendants. Just like the unicorns, the pendants represented the sun and the moon, and just like the unicorns, the twins had a special kind of connection. It was worth a shot.

They each took off their necklace and slowly approached the unicorn, reaching up nervously and placing the pendants around its neck so that they were touching.

Immediately, the two pendants clicked together like magnets and they began to glow with a golden light. The golden glow beneath the unicorn's icy prison began to shine more strongly, too. Hana and Jakob crouched down and shielded their eyes from the dazzling, magical brightness.

Eventually it dimmed, and the unicorn was no longer a statue but a living thing, its hot breath visible in the freezing air. The creature reared up, as if stretching after a long, deep sleep. Then, with its hooves clattering and skidding over the icy ground, it made for the cave's entrance.

"Quick!" Hana cried.

The twins scrambled to their feet and followed the shimmering creature to the mouth of the cave. At once, the ground began to tremble and a wonderful warmth enveloped them. Then, in front of their eyes, for the first time in a hundred years, the snow began to melt.

The twins looked around in wonder as green shoots of grass appeared and bright flowers began to carpet the hillside. Above them, the sky was blue and the sun shone.

"It's hot!" Jakob laughed. "It's actually hot." He shrugged off his thick coat and felt the warm sun on his skin for the first time in his life.

Far below, the Golden Unicorn pricked up its ears – hearing something on the wind. Suddenly, with a shake of its glistening mane, it thundered across the sun-dappled meadows in search of its mate, the Silver Unicorn. All that was left behind were two pendants, one golden sun and one silver moon, lying in a pool of melted snow. The Golden Unicorn, lost to the world for years, had returned.

The Golden and Silver were the first unicorns.

They represent the sun and the moon.

Water Moons

These unicorns live in and around water. They protect sailors in need and represent the mysteries of time.

Crystal, sapphire or coral horns

They have the longest manes and tails of all unicorns

They can gallop on water

CASE STUDY TWO:

Selena Floros

LOCATION: The Greek coast
and the Mediterranean Sea
TIME: Mid 18th century
M.U.S. STATUS: Society legend
and heroic unicorn spotter

SELWYN'S CASE NOTES:

Selena Floros – the 'Great Adventurer of Cyrus' – was a sailor and adventurer from Greece. She once ran a fleet of merchant ships across the Mediterranean Sea, which brought her vast fame and fortune.

However, Selena wasn't just a trader, she was also a keen unicorn spotter. When she was a girl, she had a dramatic encounter with the legendary Water Moon unicorns. Thanks to her, we know that some Water Moons come out in the day, not just at night, as we had once thought.

Pirates *in* Pursuit

I grabbed a sword from the deck and raised it above my head. The pirate's weapon came down to meet my own and they clanged together. The sound of crunching metal rang out across the empty skies and the crashing waves below.

Every one of the muscles in my arms tensed as I tried to hold off the scar-faced brute in front of me, but I knew my strength was fading.

"I've got you now, you squirming rat," he growled.

I gritted my teeth and held firm. I'll admit, things weren't looking good for me, the Great Adventurer of Cyrus. If I didn't do something quickly, I'd be sharing the fate of countless other sailors, dropping into the sea like a stone and resting in a watery grave.

"Not if I get you first, you barnacle-faced bully," I spat back …

*

But, wait a minute, I'm getting ahead of myself. I haven't even explained how I ended up fighting a pirate with breath like rotten fish in the first place. I should start at the beginning …

*

I'd always yearned for a life of adventure. My father was a sailor, and my older brother, Theo, was too, so the sea was in my blood. Yet they said a sailor's life wasn't for me because I was just a girl. Of course, I was determined to prove them wrong.

At the time, I lived in Cyrus, a small port town on the Greek coast. I watched every morning as the men set sail on another adventure, while I stayed at home helping to bake bread and look after the chickens in the yard. Whenever Theo returned, he would entrance me with tales of the sea. There were mermaids that tempted sailors with beautiful songs and storms whipped up by Poseidon, the god of the sea. But my favourite stories were of the sea unicorns. They were called Water Moons and were said to help sailors in trouble.

All these incredible tales – and they expected me to stay at home and bake bread! I soon decided I'd had enough of watching the sheets blowing on the line and imagining them to be sails buffeted by the wind.

It was time to have an adventure of my own.

Early one morning, under cover of darkness, I crept out of the house and followed Theo to the docks. I remember that the air was cool and scented with citrus. There was a shipment of oranges and lemons leaving that day and the men were already loading their cargo on board. I'd been on my brother's ship before, so I knew how to sneak aboard. Silently, I tiptoed past the shouting sailors and tucked myself into a hidey-hole among the boxes.

At last, the vast ship groaned to life and I watched with a mixture of uncertainty and excitement as the land, and my home, drifted further and further into the distance.

After a few hours, when I knew we were too far from the coast to return and my legs were stiff, I crawled out of my hiding space. Theo was furious to see me and demanded that the captain turn the ship around. But, luckily for me, the captain was a man who had never once delivered a late shipment and he refused to return to port.

"Let's put her to work, instead," he barked. "She can be the lookout, if she's so keen to be a sailor."

So, despite Theo's protests and the laughter of his shipmates, I scurried up to the crow's nest before the captain could change his mind.

Finally I felt like a real sailor.

I didn't really expect adventure to strike so fast, though. I'd only been on watch for a few hours, scanning the horizon, when I spotted something in the distance that didn't look right. It was a ship, not much bigger than our own, but it was moving at pace right towards us.

I squinted against the sun as the ship drew closer, and what I saw chilled the blood in my veins: a black flag was flying from the mast.

I shimmied down to the deck as quickly as I could and raised the alarm.

"Pirates!" I yelled. "Pirates on our port side!"

For a moment, the men seemed frozen to the spot, not wanting, or not able, to believe what the scrawny young girl in front of them was saying. But when the captain turned to look and then started barking orders, the deck soon burst into action. The sails were adjusted to full mast and the great ship lurched forwards through the waves.

But it was all too late.

The pirates were closing in, and in no time, they'd pulled alongside us. I stared in terror at their scruffy beards and mean faces. Some brandished swords and others yelled foul curses.

The captain ordered his crew to set course for the Caldera Pass. Hearing this, some of the men cried out in dismay. Some even threatened to mutiny, but the captain's resolve was firm.

"Mutinous dogs!" he yelled at them. "If you don't follow my orders you can join those pirates at the bottom of the sea."

This soon shut them up.

Although, I quickly discovered why the crew were so worried. The Caldera Pass ran along the coast and was a wave-battered labyrinth of craggy rocks, which jutted above the water like the crooked teeth of Poseidon himself. Charting a course through it would be full of peril.

Regardless, the ship surged forwards and we veered past the first rock with the pirates right on our tail. The sea had become a swirling whirlpool and the next rock in front of us was even bigger than the first. We were caught between the raging water, which would swallow our ship like a hungry sea monster, and a giant, jagged rock that would surely wreck us.

The pirates had caught up with us and several were able to leap on to our boat. They began fighting the crew at once, and the sound of clanging metal swords filled the air. The boat rocked violently and I was thrown to the floor. When I looked up, a rotten-breathed pirate was standing menacingly over me.

I picked up a sword that had been dropped on the deck and met him in combat. He was much stronger than me, but I was nimble and quick. I twisted my blade and caught him off balance. He stumbled to his knees and I took my chance, shoving him overboard.

"Take that, you pirate scum!" I shouted.

But he wasn't finished with me yet and grabbed my ankle as he toppled over the edge of the boat, pulling me with him.

I hit the water and began to sink, the light from above quickly fading. I didn't know what had happened to Theo, the crew or even the other pirates. All I could sense was the churning of the water and the chill creeping into my bones.

As I desperately struggled to swim back to the surface, I realized that I wasn't alone in the water. Heading straight towards me was something that my brother had often told me about – a Water Moon unicorn, the protector of sailors and the most magical creature in the sea. And there wasn't just one, but many. They were of varying colours and sizes – bright turquoises, dark blues, white like the froth on a wave and pink like coral. I'd been told they only came out by the light of the moon, but that was wrong.

The unicorn swimming gracefully towards me was pink, with a horn of coral. I was struggling to breathe, but as the unicorn came closer, magic overcame me and I was encircled in a giant bubble that allowed me to take a breath. My heart leapt as, ahead of me, I spotted Theo, smiling in his own magic bubble. It was like something straight out of the mythical tales of sailors from the past. I clambered on to the back of the pink unicorn and tightly gripped its mane.

The sea sparkled with beautiful light and colour, glistening seaweeds and a kaleidoscope of darting fish. We had obviously been lucky enough to stumble upon the beautiful home of these amazing creatures.

All too quickly, though, I felt myself rising to the surface. There was chaos all around, as the rescued sailors clambered back on board the ship and the unicorns galloped on the waves alongside us. When they saw all was well, they whinnied and disappeared under the frothing waters.

As for the pirates, their ship had been scuttled by one of the jagged rocks and we watched as the men swam desperately towards the nearby coast. Although they didn't deserve it, the

40

Water Moon unicorns helped all of the pirates who were in need, as well.

Despite the pursuit, we delivered the ship's cargo on time, which pleased the captain, and we never forgot our encounter with the Water Moons that day. The crew spoke of the strange magic of the Caldera Pass in hushed tones and one morning I woke to find the carved head of a unicorn on our ship's prow. One of the sailors must have made it during the night, in order to bring us even more good luck.

As for me, there was no way anyone could stop me sailing after that adventure. For thirty years I ran a fleet of ships across the Mediterranean, and came to be known as the Great Adventurer of Cyrus. I saw many Water Moon unicorns during my time as a sea captain and I'm writing this record now to preserve the knowledge of these gentle creatures and pass on my story. To anyone who reads this, I hope you too will look out for Water Moon unicorns and have many adventures of your own.

Shadow Nights

These ethereal unicorns are made of pure magic. They move between the spirit world, the dream world and the real world.

Their horns are made of black onyx

Silver manes and dark coats flecked with stars

Shadow Nights represent sleep and the power of dreams

CASE STUDY
THREE:

Arthur Sims

LOCATION: London, the Royal Albert Hall
TIME: Late 19th century
M.U.S. STATUS: Visionary
and unicorn dreamer

SELWYN'S CASE NOTES:
Sometimes at the M.U.S. we never know
where we'll find a unicorn story. This series
of newspaper articles was discovered in
our very own archive. They tell the story
of 'Tumbling Arty'. At the time, he was
the most famous acrobat in the world.

However, it wasn't just acrobatics
that the newspaper was interested in –
it was his encounter with a Shadow Night
and how he saved Queen Victoria's
Golden Jubilee from disaster!

A Gallop
by Gaslight

16th June 1887 – RETURNING FOR ROYALTY

Readers of the *London Chronicle* will be delighted to learn that Master Arthur Sims, well known to us all as 'Tumbling Arty', has returned to the city of his birth for an extra-special, gala performance.

Mr Sims had been touring North America, but when Her Majesty Queen Victoria asked him to perform for her Golden Jubilee, how could he possibly refuse?

Sims' celebrated troupe, the Aerial Astonishers, will join the festivities at the Royal Albert Hall on the 20th of the month, along with The Enigmatic Roderick, a master magician, and Pongo and Tibs, the most famous clowns in the world.

Mr Sims, looking smart in his three-piece suit and slicked-back hair, but somewhat tired from a troubled sea voyage, had this to say:

"I love London; there's no city in the world like it. I haven't got the words to describe the honour of performing before Her Majesty. Now, if you will excuse me, I have a routine to practise!"

We must, however, advise readers that the performance is not open to the general public, since Her Majesty's safety is of the utmost importance. A select few tickets will be offered by lottery. Of course, the *Chronicle* will also have a front seat to bring you all of the action and excitement.

17th June 1887 – VILLAINS ACCOST QUEEN

Our Queen Victoria has once again been assailed by thieves. This reporter understands that while Her Majesty was at the opera in Covent Garden, a person of ill standing disguised himself as a member of staff, with the intention to steal the very jewels that Her Majesty was wearing on her person.

We are relieved to report that a beady-eyed and brave Lady-in-Waiting stopped the ruffian before he could carry out his plan. She didn't recognize the so-called servant, and knew Queen Victoria would never authorize a new attendant to accompany her to such an important social occasion. She called for a police officer at once, at which point the criminal fled. Sadly, the constabulary, despite the lady providing them with a lengthy description, has been unable to trace the offending individual.

With the Golden Jubilee almost upon us, we at the *London Chronicle* worry that something even more bold is being planned. Are the police content to allow our Queen to be repeatedly set upon by thieves? Urgent action must be taken!

18th June 1887 – TUMBLER FUMBLES STUNT

Our reporter was invited to watch Tumbling Arty and his Aerial Astonishers this morning, as they rehearsed for the Golden Jubilee performance. What a grand spectacle it was! Seeing the graceful ladies and gentlemen hurl themselves through the air in stark defiance of gravity, one could almost believe they were fairies in flight.

Sadly, though, it seems that Tumbling Arty, the Queen's favourite, is not a well man. As he was swinging through the air, rehearsing his latest and most daring routine, he cried out and fell to the floor. Thankfully, he was not seriously hurt. But when we rushed to help assist, he said this:

"I saw it again! The black horse with a horn like a spear. It follows me wherever I go, whether I am awake or dreaming. Surely, a vision such as this cannot mean me well?"

As the rest of the performers crowded around Arty and helped him up, we noted that his forehead was damp with sweat and his expression strangely twisted. It seemed that a dream had followed him into this world, for no one else in the hall had seen any sign of a black horse, and there were certainly none performing in the show.

In a shocking statement, Gaveston, a young boy, and one of the newest Aerial Astonishers, implied that something similar had happened before.

"Master Arty's been seeing things regularly. A great black horse mostly, like a stallion from a field of war. Except, this one's got a horn sticking out of its head. By night he dreams of it and by day it haunts him, so that he becomes distracted. The rest of the troupe aren't happy; what if Master Arty should have one of his visions when he's meant to be catching us out of the air? I don't reckon Queen Victoria would be pleased to see us splatter on the ground!"

19ᵗʰ June 1887 – IT'S IN THE STARS

With the Golden Jubilee gala performance taking place tomorrow night, we bring you an exclusive report on the health of acrobat Arthur Sims.

According to Gaveston, Mr Sims is still troubled by his visions of the black, one-horned horse. But his dreams now feature the Queen herself, as well as a third individual whom Sims would only describe as a "scowling, long-legged and suspicious spider of a man."

Sims explained all of this to a mystic called Madame Hieroglyphica, also part of the troupe. The *Chronicle* understands that Hieroglyphica is a fortune teller of no small ability, and that Mr Sims was depending upon her to decipher his troubling dreams and visions. Gaveston had apparently pressed his ear to an upper window during the consultation and this is what he heard:

"Arty, this is deep magic you've stumbled into," she said. "The creature you see in your dreams is a unicorn. But it's not the sort you see on a coat of arms. This type is dark and mysterious. They're called Shadow Nights. Legends say that they pass through dreams and the waking world to bring messages or warnings. But, Arty, don't be afraid. Those who are brave enough to heed a Shadow Night will be sure to do well. Whatever the unicorn is trying to tell you, listen!"

21st June 1887 – THE BIG NIGHT

We at the *London Chronicle* can barely believe what unfolded last night at the Golden Jubilee Gala, but our readers must be informed. It seems incredible, but there is no one here who would not swear it was the truth. Our reporter was there and this is what he saw:

The events of the evening began as everyone
expected. The air buzzed with excitement; the
house was packed. An armed guard stood to
attention at the entrance and allowed no one to pass
without rigorous scrutiny. Her Majesty took her seat
at seven o'clock, wearing a sparkling diamond tiara, never
before worn in public. Such an action, it was broadly felt,
was intended to show that she would not be intimidated by
the attempts at thievery which have lately stalked her.

The band struck up and the acts took to the stage. Her Majesty
watched the magician and clowns with approval. Eventually,
it was time for the Aerial Astonishers to live up to their
proud name.

Tumbling Arty and his companion, Gaveston, swung on their
trapezes. The audience gasped as Gaveston let go, only for Arty
to snatch him up at the last minute – before throwing him back
again, giving rise to an even louder gasp. Gaveston caught hold
of his high trapeze quite easily, Arty reached his and the
audience applauded with relief and amazement.

Arty smiled to the crowd and everything seemed to be
going well. But, the next moment, the smile faltered and
Arty cried out: "The black unicorn – I see it, it calls to me!"

The band fell silent. Arthur Sims thrust out a trembling finger and all eyes in the Royal Albert Hall turned to follow his gaze. Some saw the unicorn pass by like a black cloud on the wind, others saw nothing of it at all. But either way, shrieks of horror erupted in the hall. Arty then turned and pointed to a spot directly above Her Majesty Queen Victoria. Occupying that spot, dangling from a rope strung from the rafters, was a man with spindly limbs and a mean gaze. The spotlights were turned to illuminate him, in the very act of reaching out for the Queen's diamond tiara.

Who can say what might have happened then, had Arty Sims not been there? A coward would have hesitated and questioned what they saw, but Arty Sims did not. He heeded the unicorn's warning. He swung forwards on his trapeze with all of his considerable strength and with a mighty yell that boomed around the hall, he soared through the air. Then, when he was in position, he let go of the trapeze in a daring leap and tumbled through the air, grabbing hold of the thief and plucking him from the rope.

The two men dropped to the floor like stones, whereupon Arty Sims wrestled the would-be thief to the ground. The Queen's attendants hastened to shield her from the sight of two men fighting on the floor of the royal box, throwing punches at each other. Arty held on to the man who struggled like a wriggling weasel. The police arrived and swiftly put the man into handcuffs.

Arty Sims received a standing ovation from the crowd, who couldn't have asked for a night more full of excitement. As for the man who dared to approach the Queen, he is said to reside in the dungeons now. After the performance, Her Majesty paid the performers a personal visit to convey her thanks and Arty Sims was the recipient of a special medal. It seems that the Shadow Night unicorn, black, dreamlike and good, has visited London to help us avert catastrophe. Dear readers, we should be forever grateful.

Woodland Flowers
heal and protect.

Shadow Nights
appear in dreams.

Woodland Flowers

These unicorns are gentle and kind. Magic flowers woven through their manes and tails give them powers of healing.

Twisting horn

These unicorns love nature

Woodland Flowers have the power of telepathy with animals and humans

Manes and tails filled with wild flowers

CASE STUDY FOUR:

Lizzie Elms

LOCATION: Manhattan, New York, USA
TIME: Modern day
M.U.S. STATUS: Society member,
unicorn spotter and recorder

SELWYN'S CASE NOTES:

Unicorns aren't often sighted in cities,
let alone one of the busiest in the world.
Lizzie Elms was just 12 years old when she
discovered a magical corner of Central Park,
where Woodland Flowers roam free.

Lizzie has a deep love of wildlife and
animals, a quality that Woodland Flowers
can sense in humans. After her encounter,
she made sure to tell the American branch
of the M.U.S., so they could keep a watchful
eye over these unicorns and make sure
they were protected.

The Unicorns
of Central Park

Lizzie Elms found her favourite tree in the whole
park – a majestic old oak – and sat down
under its branches, shaded from the afternoon
sunshine. She pulled a library book from her
backpack and licked salt off the big, soft pretzel
she'd bought from a street cart on the way.

Surrounded by gleaming skyscrapers, Central Park was a green oasis amid the hustle and bustle of New York City. Lizzie loved to come here after school – especially in springtime, when cheerful yellow daffodils dotted the grass and frothy pink blossom made the trees look like candyfloss.

A flash of bright red feathers caught her eye as a bird swooped overhead. "A cardinal!" Lizzie gasped. She took out her notebook to record yet another creature she'd spotted in the park. She'd already seen chipmunks, skunks, groundhogs and all kinds of birds over the last few weeks.

Leaning back against the tree, she opened up her book – a guide to magical creatures and where they lived. As she munched her pretzel and listened to the starlings chattering, Lizzie read about Spirit Owls, who protected nocturnal animals, Silver Squirrels, who looked after trees, and Forest Guardians, foxes that kept woodlands safe. But her favourites were the Woodland Flowers – a special type of unicorn with healing powers.

Looking up from her book, Lizzie noticed a squirrel's beady eyes watching her curiously. "Hey, there, fuzzy face," Lizzie whispered softly. The squirrel twitched its nose but didn't run away. Animals always trusted Lizzie; it was as if they could sense how much she loved them.

I wish you really could do magic, Lizzie thought, tossing the grateful squirrel the last bite of her pretzel.

Noticing she was late, Lizzie scrambled to her feet. She shoved the book into her backpack and hurried off, stopping along the way to pick up chocolate bar wrappers, crisp packets and plastic drink bottles and put them in a bin. Lizzie hated to see litter, especially somewhere as beautiful as Central Park.

"Hi, Lizzie!" called an older woman wearing dungarees and gardening clogs as Lizzie arrived, panting, at the Central Park Community Garden.

"Hi, Jan," gasped Lizzie, catching her breath. "What do you need me to do today?"

Jan was the head gardener and Lizzie's mum's best friend. She'd taught Lizzie, who volunteered at the community garden, everything she knew about plants and flowers.

"Hmm," said Jan, wiping her brow, leaving a smudge of dirt across her forehead. "There's so much to do I hardly know where to begin. Why don't we start by weeding the butterfly garden?"

Last summer, Lizzie had helped Jan design a special garden with flowers to attract pollinators. They'd planted lavender,

hollyhocks and fragrant herbs like mint
and sage, hoping that the sweet-smelling, colourful
plants, would attract bees and butterflies. But
now the garden looked straggly, and no insects were
buzzing around the plants.

Pulling on a pair of gardening gloves, Lizzie knelt down by the
edge of the flowerbed and got to work. She dug up bindweed
and yanked up a sticky vine.

"Is this a weed?" she asked Jan, pointing her spade at a prickly-
looking plant.

"No," said Jan, shaking her head. "That's a thistle, but it hasn't
flowered yet. The butterfly garden just isn't thriving, I'm afraid."

"Ugh!" said Lizzie, holding up a plastic fizzy drink holder that
had got tangled in a plant's stem.

Jan took a pair of clippers out of her tool belt and snipped
through the plastic rings. "These are dangerous – they can
strangle birds and animals."

Lizzie's stomach twisted at the thought of an animal getting
hurt. "All this litter can't be good for the plants, either," she said
sadly, picking a plastic bag out of the flowerbed.

She wished the creatures in her book were real.
If magical animals really existed, they could bring
the butterfly garden back to life.

When she'd finished weeding the bed and watering the
vegetable patch, it was time for Lizzie to go home. But just
before she did, a silvery-gold butterfly flew past out of nowhere.
Lizzie smiled. At least there was one butterfly in the garden.

"Bye!" she called to Jan before heading off through the woods.

"Bye, Lizzie," Jan called. "Say hello to your mum for me."

As Lizzie walked through the trees, late afternoon sunshine
peeked through the leaves. Far off in the distance, Lizzie could
hear the honking of rush-hour traffic. Suddenly, the silvery-gold
butterfly fluttered into view again. Animals did always love her,
but this butterfly was really keen to get her attention.

"What do you want, mister?" Lizzie laughed.

As if in reply, the butterfly stopped and perched on a branch.
Lizzie reached out to touch it but immediately leapt back.

"Ouch!" she cried, looking down at the drop of blood on her
hand. She'd prickled herself on a thorn. She looked up and saw

that the butterfly was fluttering further into the foliage, flitting from leaf to leaf.

"Hey!" she cried. "You could've warned me it was prickly."

As she spoke, something silently stepped out from behind a thicket of bushes. Lizzie gasped. The creature had a velvety brown coat and stood tall and proud, and the butterfly had led her right to it.

Staring at her with wise, chocolate-coloured eyes, the animal slowly stepped closer and Lizzie saw red roses and other magical-looking flowers woven into its mane.

It was a unicorn!

Lizzie trembled as the unicorn lowered its head. A petal fell from a flower on its mane and on to her palm, and instantly her cut was healed. Lizzie reached out and gently stroked the unicorn's silky brown mane in thanks. It was just like the Woodland Flowers in her library book. The unicorn bowed its head and trotted deeper into the woods, its heart-shaped hooves silent on the mossy ground. Lizzie had to follow, to see where the magical creature would go.

The unicorn led her to a distant corner of the park that seemed to crackle with magic. The air shimmered and stretched around them, like a giant soap bubble until – POP! – they suddenly broke through. Blinking in astonishment, Lizzie found herself in the most beautiful garden she had ever seen.

Roses in every shade imaginable formed arches around the edge of the garden, filling the air with their sweet perfume. There were bushes shaped like birds and hearts, and flowerbeds bursting with colourful blossoms – from dahlias and delphiniums to pansies and petunias. There were flowers Lizzie had never seen before with rainbow-coloured petals. In the very centre of the garden, giant water lilies with enormous purple flowers floated on a pond, where a unicorn was drinking.

Other unicorns were busy tending the plants. One unicorn touched its horn to a bush and flowers shaped like blue trumpets instantly blossomed. Another unicorn pawed at the ground with its hooves and a vine with bright red leaves magically sprang up from the soil.

Lizzie's unicorn led her around the garden, past bearberry bushes with juicy red berries, vibrant orchids and spiky agave plants. She recognized them all from her book about magical creatures: these plants were just what unicorns liked to eat. For the rest of the afternoon, Lizzie snipped and pruned alongside

the Woodland Flowers, who delicately tended to the plants and flowers that grew in their garden.

"You're so lucky," she said. "Magic makes your garden look very, very beautiful."

It isn't just magic that makes our garden grow, the Woodland Flower replied. *It's all of us caring for it together.*

Lizzie was shocked. The unicorn had spoken straight into her mind! She wished she could stay longer, but the sun had begun to set and she knew her mum would worry if she didn't get home soon. "I've got to go now," she said reluctantly, "but thank you for the most magical afternoon."

We are grateful for your help, Lizzie, said the Woodland Flower. He shook his head, and seeds from the flowers woven into his mane fell into Lizzie's hands. *And in return, I hope these seeds may bring some magic to your garden ...*

Two weeks later a banner reading "Welcome to our Open Day!" fluttered above the entrance to the community garden. Volunteers were busy picking up litter, watering the flowerbeds and hoeing the vegetable patch.

66

"What a great idea to organize an open day," said a man pushing a wheelbarrow full of compost.

"It was all Lizzie's idea," said Jan.

Not quite, thought Lizzie. The Woodland Flowers had inspired her to do it.

The day after she'd met the unicorns, Lizzie had secretly scattered the magical seeds in the community garden. Plants had sprung up overnight, their flowers now blooming in a riot of colour and in combinations the gardeners had never seen before. Bees buzzed from blossom to blossom, collecting pollen, while butterflies fluttered in the air, their wings matching the yellow and orange marigolds. The Central Park Community Garden was flourishing and today lots of people had signed up as volunteers, to keep it that way forever.

"Wow!" said Jan, gazing around the garden proudly. "It's amazing what teamwork can accomplish."

Glancing over at the woodland, Lizzie thought she could see a twisted horn peeking out from behind the trees. *Yes*, she thought, with a secret smile. *Teamwork ... and a sprinkling of unicorn magic!*

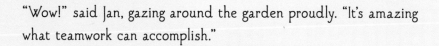

Ice Wanderers

Ice Wanderers live in cold climates. They can communicate across vast distances with magical light.

White coats that sparkle with magic

Horns made of ice or pearl

Ice Wanderers represent endurance and resilience

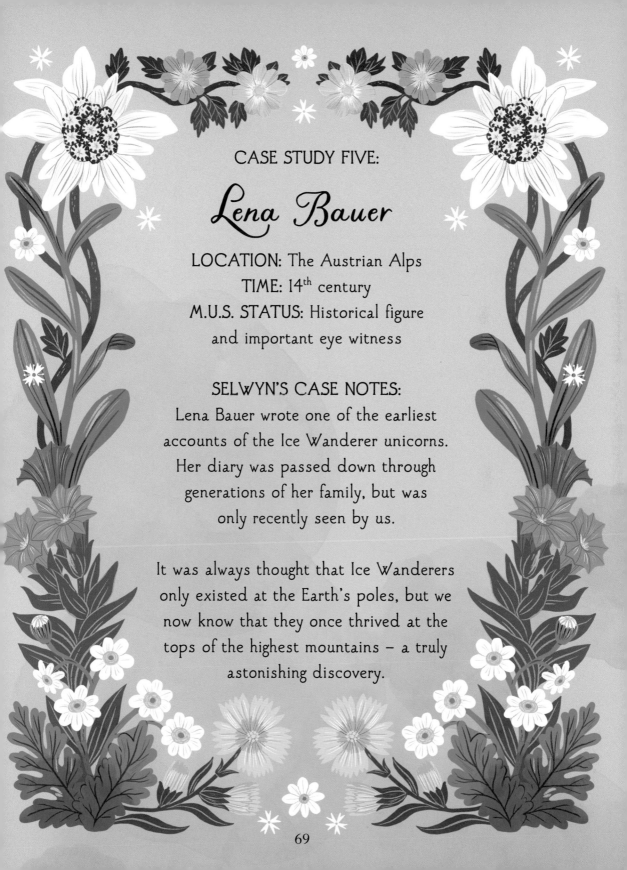

CASE STUDY FIVE:

Lena Bauer

LOCATION: The Austrian Alps
TIME: 14th century
M.U.S. STATUS: Historical figure
and important eye witness

SELWYN'S CASE NOTES:
Lena Bauer wrote one of the earliest
accounts of the Ice Wanderer unicorns.
Her diary was passed down through
generations of her family, but was
only recently seen by us.

It was always thought that Ice Wanderers
only existed at the Earth's poles, but we
now know that they once thrived at the
tops of the highest mountains – a truly
astonishing discovery.

The Flight
of the Unicorns

TUESDAY 5th – SOUTHERN MOUNTAINS

I put on my warmest boots and left camp
this morning to begin my search for the Ice
Wanderer unicorns. The weather was fair and
warm in the foothills, but I knew there'd
be harsher conditions to come higher up.

There have always been rumours of these unicorns living in the icy peaks of the Alps. Goat herders and brave travellers who cross the mountains know all about their strength and stamina. They speak of creatures with pearl horns, immune to the cold, with the strength of ten horses and the power to communicate over long distances. The General decided that these unicorns would make a great addition to his army.

I don't much enjoy being a scout in General Krumm's Alpine forces, but there isn't a lot of choice when you're from Alterhaus. Krumm's fortress, perched high on the slope, is the base from which he controls the Southern Mountains with an iron fist. Everyone lives to serve the fortress and, more importantly, the General, who has grown fat with greed and mean with power.

"Lena," he barked at me, just yesterday, "a peasant girl like you, born in the mountains, will surely know where to look for the Ice Wanderers. Find them for me."

I answered with a simple, "Yes, Sir!" It was clear I had no choice.

Today, as the green grass and gentle warmth of the low hills gave way to the bitter winds and icy ground of the taller peaks, I cursed General Krumm's name. Now, as I settle down for the night, all alone, beside a fire with my sheepskin around me, I hope to chronicle these elusive creatures.

WEDNESDAY 6th – ICE RIDGE

This morning I woke with frost on my eyelashes. The weather had worsened and the snow was coming down in thick flakes. With the fire long dead, I danced on the spot to warm myself – doing my own silly version of the local *schuhplattler* dance. A curious mountain goat looked at me as if I'd lost my mind. This strange and chilly start to the day, though, was going to give way to something more exciting.

I found a stream that hadn't yet frozen over and drank deeply from it, splashing my face for good measure to wake myself up. It was there that I noticed a thicket of half-chewed silver posies growing on the bank, and realized I was on the right track. I'd been reliably informed that this sturdy winter plant was the Ice Wanderers' favourite food.

I followed the stream uphill, until the air began to thin and looking down made me feel dizzy. Even for a 'mountain peasant', the height of the peak thrilled me. As I continued up the icy slope, I saw pink and yellow lights flash above me in the sky. It was something I'd heard of but never seen: Ice Wanderer magic.

I'd stumbled upon a unicorn gathering. They stood before me, knocking horns in greeting and stamping their hooves, whereupon a great trembling shook the mountainside. I now understood

why they were said to accidentally create avalanches. I was captivated by the beauty of their pearly white coats, and the pink and yellow magic that flowed from them in waves. It enveloped the unicorns like steam rising from a hot spring.

The only problem is that I will have to tell General Krumm what I have found. I know he will be pleased, but deep down something doesn't feel right.

THURSDAY 7th – FROM THE ALTERHAUS DUNGEON

Just as I'd predicted, Krumm's eyes lit up when I told him.

"At last!" he cried. "They're mine. And with the Ice Wanderer unicorns in my forces, there's nothing to stop me from conquering the entire valley. Alterhaus is just the beginning. Next, we move on to Queen Sofia's castle, and then I'll be the ultimate ruler of the mountains."

What I couldn't have predicted, though, was that I'd be writing this entry from the dungeons of Alterhaus. I had better start from the beginning ...

The morning after I'd trekked back down the mountain and told Krumm of my discovery, the whole of Alterhaus became a hive of activity. There was no time to lose. Horses were saddled up, men began to change into chainmail and armour, and flags were held high ready for the expedition. Within hours we were back out on the slopes and heading straight for the unicorns.

Krumm led the expedition, his poor steed not only straining under his vast bulk, but being whipped whenever it showed signs of slowing. The General's face was twisted with glee, yet his men were tense and nervous. It was dangerous to bring horses so high up into the mountains. Also, the men knew that if they didn't catch the unicorns and bend them to Krumm's will, they would be severely punished. And no one wanted to spend the rest of their lives, rotting away in the frozen dungeons of Alterhaus. I should know.

On horseback, the mountain trek was much quicker and easier. I rode on a soldier's horse, clinging on behind him, which gave me a terrifying view of the treacherously steep mountainside that fell below us. The soldier wore thick armour and carried a menacing-looking sword, and in his saddlebags there were nets made of strong cord. I pitied the beautiful unicorns, who were to become mere warhorses in Krumm's army.

Following my directions, Krumm and his men quickly found the stream with the beautiful silver posies, and the unicorns grazing on its banks.

"By the gods!" Krumm exclaimed. Several of his men gasped as well. They'd heard the stories but never expected to see such magnificent beasts. "They will be fine fighting machines, I have no doubt about it."

"They're not made for fighting," I protested under my breath.

The unicorns were skittish and nervous, but brave. Seeing the army, one of them stamped on the ground, sending a shudder through the mountainside. Krumm ordered an advance, and we all edged forwards, but before we could get anywhere near them, the unicorns fled with some speed.

"After them, you rock-headed fools!" Krumm cried. "Catch them and bring them to me or you'll never see the light of day again."

We raced after them, the sound of scrambling hooves and the whinnies from our horses echoing off the steep mountainsides. The drumming of the unicorns' hooves, combined with those of our horses, caused the mountain to tremble, and snow began cascading all around us. Several of the men were swept off their saddles and sent tumbling to their doom.

"Faster, you brutes, faster!" Krumm demanded.

The soldier in front of me reached out to grab his net, but before he could, I unhooked the saddlebag, so it fell to the ground with a dull thud.

"Curse you, Lena!" he cried. "You'll go to the dungeon for that."

I didn't care – the unicorns didn't deserve the gruelling life that would await them in Krumm's army.

But my ploy had not worked, and eventually the unicorns were herded down the mountain and on to softer terrain. We were heading back towards the Alterhaus. Just as we approached the bridge that spans the valley, I noticed some of Krumm's soldiers from the fortress riding to meet us.

As the unicorns reached the middle of the bridge, with soldiers in front and soldiers behind, something magical happened. They stomped their hooves as one and the ancient stone bridge began to wobble under our feet. Cracks appeared in the cobbled road, and the bridge heaved and shook like an old tree about to be felled. The valley floor began to look a very long way down and the bridge didn't feel sturdy at all.

As the men on both sides of the beasts stepped back, a magical light of pink and yellow rose out of nowhere – just like I'd seen earlier on the mountain. Before our eyes, the unicorns

changed into spirit beings. Instead of the flesh and blood creatures I'd seen previously, they looked like they were made of clouds of magic. I heard one soldier whispering under his breath about the legendary 'Air Wanderers' – Ice Wanderers that could transform into clouds.

Krumm was furious and ordered yet another futile advance. But before the men could move a muscle, the Air Wanderers leapt off the bridge and into the air, cantering off on the wind. At the same time, the bridge finally gave way and began to crumble into the valley below. We had no option but to retreat, as the ancient stones plummeted through the air and the bridge vanished before our eyes.

Days later, Krumm's fury has still not subsided and I write this entry from a dismal cell in the Alterhaus. According to him, it was my fault. According to him, I should've known about the unicorns' magic. What's more, I should have taken the chance to capture them, not to loosen the net on the soldier's horse.

I now find myself chained to the dungeon wall by my ankle, with other unfortunates who had got on the wrong side of his anger, with little chance of escape.

SUNDAY 10th – HOME – A MIRACLE

I'm free, and General Krumm's reign is over. I can hardly believe it, but it's true.

It was from my cell that I saw Queen Sofia's army advancing. Sensing the weakness of General Krumm, she had sent them to storm the Alterhaus and they had done so with speed. Out of the iron-clad window of my cell, I saw them approach.

The army wasted no time ransacking the fortress. It turned out that General Krumm's army wasn't the fighting machine he boasted of it being, and that poorly fed men didn't make for happy soldiers. When Sofia's forces prevailed, the other prisoners and I were free, and I can't say I wasn't glad. After that day, there was a greater feeling of freedom in the valley and no one remained under the misery of General Krumm's rule.

As for the Air Wanderers, they've never been seen since. I'm relieved, though, that they escaped, and I can only hope that their magic lives on. Every time I see a low cloud brightened by the sun's rays, I think of those magical spirits of the air galloping away on the breeze.

Come thunder or lightning, sunshine or rain,

Unicorn magic can never be tamed.

Storm Chasers

These unicorns have control over the elements, from the rains and the winds to lightning and thunder.

Horns can be star-yellow quartz, jade, opal or stone

There are four types of Storm Chaser: Storm, Sunshine, Snow and Shifter

Manes and tails that crackle with electricity

Storm Chasers represent strong emotions and they have power over the elements

CASE STUDY SIX:

Amber Li and Jun Zhao

LOCATION: China
TIME: Modern day and distant past
M.U.S. STATUS: Amber Li is an
important source and Jun Zhao is
an intriguing mythical figure

SELWYN'S CASE NOTES:
Amber Li is a young girl from Shanghai.
She was once more interested in video games
than unicorn magic, but then she heard about
Jun Zhao and the Storm Chasers.

Jun Zhao lived in China a thousand years
ago, where there was once magic in the air.
Little did Amber know that she was the
heir to a small fragment of that magic ...

The Day
of the Storm

Rain pelted down from the slate-coloured
sky. Amber Li watched the droplets
stream down the living room window.
In the park opposite an empty swing
was rocked by the howling wind.
"Hurray for Saturday!" she joked.

"Hmm, it's a bit blustery isn't it?" her grandmother laughed, joining Amber at the window. A flash of lightning was reflected in her bright eyes and a smile crinkled her mouth. "But I always think there's something fun about a storm, don't you?"

"Not when you want to play football," Amber sighed. "I suppose I could always play online ..."

"Ah well, before you do," her gran began, "I want to give you something."

Amber's gran rummaged around in her bag and handed her a small gift wrapped in tissue paper. Amber carefully unfolded it, finding a cold, hard fragment of pottery inside. Painted on it in dark blue was the front half of a leaping unicorn, beating its hooves on a cloud.

"Thanks, Gran," Amber said, confused. "But what is it? And where's it from — a vase?"

"Yes," her gran said. "But not just any vase. It's the last surviving fragment of a vase that once belonged to the Jewelled Duchess. It was inside this vase that she kept the power of the Storm Chaser unicorns."

86

"Who's the Jewelled Duchess?" Amber asked, suddenly curious. "And what's a Storm Chaser unicorn?"

"Shall I tell you the legend?" her gran asked.

Amber nodded and curled up on the sofa alongside her gran. It wasn't long before the story took her away from the honking cars and pouring rain outside to ancient temple rooftops and towering mountains far away.

*

In the distant past, there was a quiet town nestled in a lush valley, flanked by great mountains. The farmers worked hard in the fields, the priests prayed in the temples and the merchants haggled in the markets. Everything stayed happily in its place. Night followed day and the seasons turned.

For a boy called Jun, his place in life was to do everything his mother told him without complaint. He collected eggs, chopped wood, washed the sheets and swept the floors. When he wasn't at home, he worked as a blacksmith's apprentice.

Until, one year, when things changed. At the beginning of summer, the weather, which was normally calm and sunny, had given way to howling storms. At noon, the sky would turn as dark as night.

Rain gushed from gutters and flooded the streets. Bolts of lightning spat across the sky – one even split an ancient willow tree to the root. People began to think the town was cursed.

"The unicorns," Jun said to his mother one rainy afternoon, as he watched his neighbour's cart floating past. "Didn't they always look after the weather?"

"Yes," his mother replied. "The Storm Chasers keep the elements in their place. At least, that's what people say."

Jun had a feeling that there was truth in the old stories. He listened carefully to what people said in the fields, the temples and the markets. There was talk that the Duchess, whose thirst for riches and greed for possessions was legendary, might have something to do with the turbulent weather conditions. She lived in a palace that clung to the mountainside and there were whisperings that she had recently acquired a quartet of beautiful horses with strange powers.

Jun, curious to see if these rumours were true, decided to find out for himself. The next day, he gathered his blacksmith's tools and climbed the mountain path up to the Duchess's palace. When he arrived, he explained to the guards that he was there to shoe her horses with the finest silver, having heard stories of their special nature. Knowing that this would please the

Duchess, who loved anyone bearing gifts, the guards decided to let the young blacksmith's apprentice enter.

He was led to a small paddock, hidden behind high walls and screened by layers of semi-translucent paper in timber frames. There, four splendid creatures lay on the grass – not horses, but unicorns – one grey, one golden-yellow, one pure white and one that shifted colour depending which way the breeze blew. Although they were beautiful, the unicorns seemed sad. One slowly munched on some hay, another glanced wearily up at Jun, then lay its head on the ground.

"These must be the Storm Chasers," Jun gasped. "The yellow Sunshine unicorn, the grey Storm, the white Snow and the grey and white Shifter. No wonder the weather is all upside down!"

"That's right, boy," a voice behind him barked. Jun jumped and spun around. The Duchess stood in front of him, dripping with jewels and gold. "And what of it?" she said. "Why are you here amongst my possessions?"

Jun composed himself, took a deep breath, and bravely replied. "I heard that there were unicorns here and I wanted to bring them a gift of new shoes. But I can see that these unicorns hardly deserve the name. Where is their magic? Why do they not play and frolic as the legends tell us? Isn't it the unicorns' play that keeps the seasons turning as they should? No wonder the weather is disturbed."

"Their magic," the Duchess laughed, coldly, "is mine now. I can do with it as I please." She led Jun to an alcove that smelt of bitter incense. A tall vase stood in a quiet corner, decorated with intricate patterns. It overflowed with blue tendrils of fizzing energy and showers of golden sparks.

At once, Jun understood that the Duchess was some kind of witch, and that the woes of the valley were entirely of her creation. She had stolen the Storm Chasers' magic and, as a result, floods, storms and heatwaves tormented the townsfolk. The unicorns were in great peril – without their magic they would continue to sicken and eventually they would die.

"Give me the vase," he said bravely. "Otherwise the valley will be tormented forever."

The Duchess laughed again, and the sound was as harsh and icy as the frost-bitten mountaintops. "Give it up? You are amusing, boy. Why would I do such a thing?"

Jun thought she might ask that and was ready. "For silver, Duchess." He quickly opened his bag to show the glinting metal inside. The Duchess lunged forwards, eager as she always was for more riches. Jun quickly pulled the bag closed, though, so she couldn't get a proper glimpse. He didn't want her to see that the glinting was merely from his common smithing tools.

The Duchess laughed a third time, and the sound was chillier than the icicles left in a Snow unicorn's wake.

"Well, what's pottery when I could have silver?" Her jewellery jangled as she spoke. "I will ask you a riddle. If you can solve it, the vase is yours."

"And if I cannot?" Jun asked.

"Then I shall take your silver, make you my servant and keep you and the unicorns here forever."

Jun shuddered, but knew he had to be brave. "Ask your riddle."

"Very well," the Duchess began. "I may be a fork, but never a knife. I may be a sheet, but never a bed. And you may hear me long after I have spoken. What am I?"

Poor Jun felt his mind was as empty as a gambler's purse. He racked his brains for the answer, but none came. In desperation he looked to the unicorns. And there, in the eye of the Storm Unicorn, he saw a deep flash, a glimmer of hope, a flicker of ...

"Lightning," he cried, suddenly understanding. "It can be forked, it can be a sheet and you only hear its 'voice', thunder, after the flash has 'spoken'."

The Duchess gave a piercing scream that echoed across the courtyard, causing the vase to shatter into a thousand pieces. The magic flowed outwards and back towards the Storm Chaser unicorns. They leapt to their feet and shook their manes, standing proud and strong. The Storm Unicorn reared up and slammed its hooves down on the ground and, with a thunderous crash, the walls of the castle fell in on themselves.

Jun watched with delight as the unicorns galloped out into the fields. They cantered up the side of a hill, and when they reached the crest, they kept going. They gradually moved into the flank of a great white cloud ... and then they were gone.

"Woah," Jun gasped.

Of the Duchess there was no trace. When her castle collapsed, she had fled to whatever shadowy dominions a vanquished witch goes to hide. Jun took a single fragment of the vase as proof of his story and returned home, enjoying the feel of sunshine that now bathed the landscape ...

*

"And that fragment is what you're holding now," Amber's gran finished. "Passed down through generations of our family."

Amber grasped it tightly. "So, the old china vase held the unicorns' magic? And it's all gone back to them now?"

"Almost all," her gran said.

"What do you mean?" Amber asked.

"Let's see." She took the fragment and held it between her clasped hands. "It really is a shame for you to be stuck at home today, all because of a rainstorm. I think a change in the weather is called for. I'm sure the Storm Chasers wouldn't mind."

She leant forwards and whispered something that sounded like a magic spell. Then there was a brief drumming sound from above, like heavy rain on the roof. Or hooves.

"Gran!" Amber cried out. "Look!"

Outside the skies had cleared and the sun was shining.

Her gran smiled. "I thought that there might be a little bit of magic left!"

Mountain Jewels and Desert Flames

Mountain Jewels are sturdy, with powers of long life.
Desert Flames are super fast, and also have the power of flight.

Mountain Jewels' horns are made of coral or opal

Desert Flames' twisting horns are made of bronze

Mountain Jewels are strong and loyal. Desert Flames help those in need.

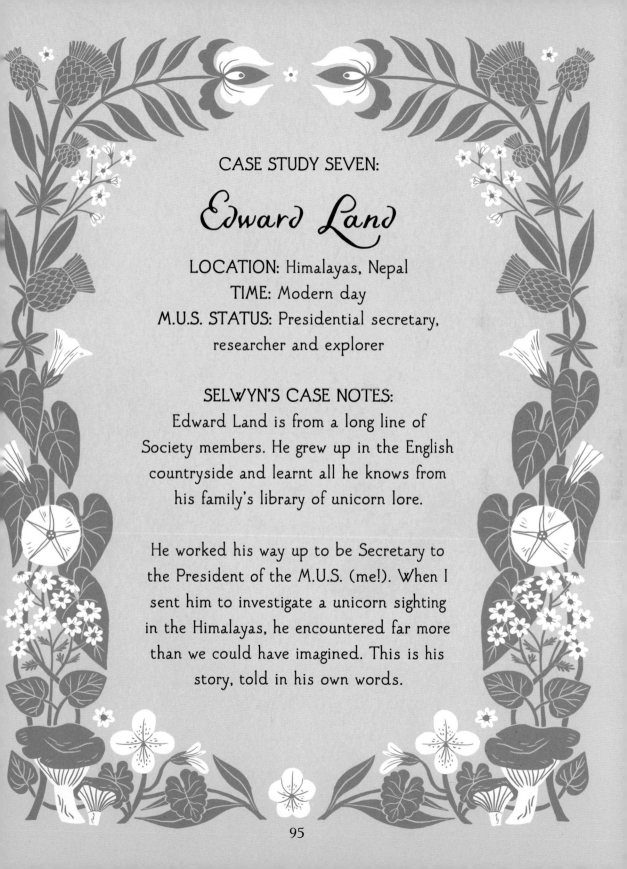

CASE STUDY SEVEN:

Edward Land

LOCATION: Himalayas, Nepal
TIME: Modern day
M.U.S. STATUS: Presidential secretary,
researcher and explorer

SELWYN'S CASE NOTES:

Edward Land is from a long line of
Society members. He grew up in the English
countryside and learnt all he knows from
his family's library of unicorn lore.

He worked his way up to be Secretary to
the President of the M.U.S. (me!). When I
sent him to investigate a unicorn sighting
in the Himalayas, he encountered far more
than we could have imagined. This is his
story, told in his own words.

The Meeting *of the* Seven Families

REPORT 371 – STRICTLY CONFIDENTIAL.
EDWARD LAND. LONDON BRANCH.

The Society has been aware of several Golden Unicorn sightings over the past fifty or sixty years. However, we've never had any definitive proof and we've always been wary of such tales.

After all, the story of the Golden and Silver Unicorns was always believed to be just that: a story. It was passed down to us over the centuries, and it was never possible to prove that these unicorns actually existed.

However, as sightings grew and grew, the Magical Unicorn Society decided to investigate. As secretary to the President, I was lucky enough to be chosen for the job. The surprising findings of my expedition, and all background details, are presented to Society members in this report. What I witnessed will change what we know about unicorns forever.

✳

I began my investigation in the extensive library of the M.U.S. London headquarters. It was there, amongst the thousands of books, cuttings and dusty old files, that I found a reference to a pair of twins, Hana and Jakob Alson. They were the first of a handful of people to have reported seeing the Golden Unicorn in the last century.

They are old now, having had their encounter when they were just children. However, when I finally managed to track them down, they remembered their sighting as if it had happened only yesterday. They spotted the Golden Unicorn in Norway, but there have been other sightings in Eastern Europe and Central

Asia. And what was even more exciting, was that these people had encountered the Golden Unicorn with the Silver Unicorn. If they and others were to be believed – and everything pointed towards them telling the truth – the mythical Golden and Silver Unicorns are back in the world.

*

I come from a long line of unicorn spotters and trackers. My mother spotted the first Woodland Flower ever to be recorded in England. My great-grandmother was the first person to make the distinction between different unicorns' hoof prints. She catalogued, for instance, the fact that Mountain Jewels have a triangular-shaped inner hoof, whereas Desert Flames have a flame-shaped hoof print.

My family told me all about their various encounters with unicorns and I was desperate to follow in their footsteps. I used to spend hours exploring the woods near my home tracking wildlife, but pretending I was on the hunt for a unicorn. I once found a badger's sett, and another time a hedgehog's burrow – not quite a Storm Chaser with a lightning-yellow mane, but it was all good practice.

As soon as I was old enough, I went to work for the Magical Unicorn Society. For years I made cups of tea and ran errands

for the older researchers and spotters. Eventually, I was trusted enough to be sent on my very own expedition – and it was an exciting mission.

Various unicorn families had been found in the foothills of the Himalayas, including Mountain Jewels and Desert Flames. It wasn't unusual for Mountain Jewels to be seen there; after all, they're perfectly suited to the terrain. They're sturdy creatures that can survive freezing temperatures and icy winds. However, Desert Flames rarely stray into such cold climates. They much prefer warm countries and, as their name implies, sandy deserts. The fact that they were seen together was also very unusual and the Society intended to find out more.

Luckily for me I was chosen to investigate this strange event, as well as a recent Golden Unicorn sighting in the area. I packed my bag and tracking essentials and, with some trepidation, was finally on the trail.

*

When I arrived in Nepal, I met with a local guide who put me on the right track. His name was Imay and he was head of the local branch of the Magical Unicorn Society. He had long been acquainted with Mountain Jewel unicorns and knew all the best places to spot them. He was the one who passed on the information about the Desert Flame sighting. He had kind eyes that looked full of wisdom and a long, neat beard. He seemed calm and polite when we met in public but as soon as we were inside, away from any prying eyes or nosey people listening in to our conversation, he became animated.

"My friend," he began, "it isn't just Mountain Jewels I've seen, and it isn't even just Desert Flames, either. I swear on my life – I have seen each type of unicorn pass through this village in the last few weeks. It's more families of unicorns than anyone has seen together in living memory!"

"But why are they meeting here?" I wondered out loud.

"Well," he began. "They may be up to something magical. They are unicorns after all ..."

I was excited by this possibility. I knew that, coupled with the Golden Unicorn sightings over the years, I was on to something momentous. Two families meeting was one thing, but all seven families at once? It had never been heard of.

The next morning I set off, taking the path that Imay had suggested, and it wasn't long before, scrambling amongst the rocks, I caught sight of a herd of Mountain Jewels that were making their way up the slope.

They had impressive horns and their sturdy frames were making light work of the stony mountain trail. Some of them noticed me, but they didn't seem bothered by my presence. They let me walk amongst them and I even stroked one unicorn's mane. However, when the climb became tougher, they left me far behind. By the time I caught up with them, the path had tailed off and my way was blocked by a huge, rushing waterfall. I had no idea where the unicorns had gone.

All I could do was sit and wait, in the hope they would return. I made myself as comfortable as possible, setting up camp and preparing something to eat. I had almost fallen asleep when I felt a presence behind me. It was a Woodland Flower – obviously very far from home. I couldn't understand what it was doing so far up the mountain, but I knew then that Imay was right – more than one unicorn family was here.

"Help yourself," I whispered, as the Woodland Flower came close enough to snatch a little of my food. However, it didn't stay with me long and was quickly on its way. This time, however, I wasn't about to let the unicorn out of my sight. I jumped up, quickly put out my campfire and followed it towards the waterfall.

Amazingly, the unicorn didn't stop when it reached the thundering wall of water. It went straight through the churning froth and tumbling cascade, disappearing from sight.

I did the only thing a good unicorn explorer could do — I went straight in after it.

*

I walked up to the waterfall and held a hand out into the spray. The water sparkled silver and gold, but when I pulled my hand back, it was completely dry. Taking a deep breath, I ventured further forwards and stepped fully through the raging water, gold and silver bursts of light clouding my vision.

When I got to the other side, I entered what I can only describe as a magical land, full of unicorns. There were Ice Wanderers and Woodland Flowers, Desert Flames and Water Moons; each one so very far from home. The scene reminded me of something I'd come across in an old file I'd found in the Magical Unicorn Society's archive. The document had described the different families of unicorns meeting up to restore their magic. I wondered if I had accidentally stumbled upon such a ceremony. Imay was right — so many unicorns in one place had to mean something magical was happening.

I caught sight of the Golden and Silver Unicorns — two unicorns that I thought I would never see with my own eyes. They stomped around impatiently, as if scolding the others for being slow to arrive.

The creatures greeted each other by gently touching horns and stamping their feet. A flicker of lightning coursed through the sky, courtesy of a Storm Chaser. An Ice Wanderer sent out pink and yellow lights, like an aurora, to accompany it.

Eventually, the greetings stopped and the Golden and Silver Unicorns took control of the proceedings. They trotted around in a circle, amongst the 'blessing' – that special group of unicorns. The light was beginning to fade in the mountains, and the sky had turned a pinky-purple. When the sun dipped below the horizons, the Golden and Silver Unicorns bowed their heads to the ground. Magical sparks leapt up from where their horns touched the earth. The other unicorn families quickly followed their lead.

Magic poured down from the sky in the form of bright flashes and coloured clouds. The Desert Flames' fiery manes glowed brighter and the stars on the Shadow Nights' hooves flickered with ever brighter light. They all glowed with a special kind of magical light. It seemed as if their magic powers were being renewed.

After a few minutes of enchantment, all was calm. The sparks had died down and the bright flashes had faded. Then, something even more incredible occurred. Another unicorn, a type I'd never seen before, walked from the waterfall behind

me. It had a pale blue coat, a dark blue mane with pink tips and a bright yellow horn made of some sort of gemstone. It was a brand-new unicorn, created when the power of all the other unicorn families was joined together. This was something that had never been documented, or even heard of, in the history of the Magical Unicorn Society.

I was left stunned, as each of the unicorn families acknowledged the new arrival, welcoming it into their special group. They bowed their heads in greeting, touching the floor once more with their horns.

In time, though, they all went back through the waterfall and into the real world. I followed, and tracked the new creature for the remainder of the night, trying to note as much about it as I could. The last glimpse I got of the unique creature was just as the sun was rising over the horizon.

I am writing this report now to let everyone in the M.U.S. know that there is a new unicorn in the world: I propose that it should be called the Dawn Spirit.

Beneath the crashing of the magical waterfall,

A new family of unicorns was born ...

Dawn Spirits

Dawn Spirits represent hope, happiness and new beginnings.
They also grant wishes to those who need them most.

Horns made of
yellow diamond

Dawn Spirits can
live in hot or
cold climates

Their manes
shimmer with the
colours of
the dawn

CASE STUDY EIGHT:

Chloe Durand

LOCATION: Brittany, France
TIME: Modern day
M.U.S. STATUS: The youngest member
to meet the eighth unicorn family

SELWYN'S CASE NOTES:

When I heard that there was a new unicorn
family, I was determined to find out more.
But it was a young girl called Chloe Durand
who had the first real encounter outside
of Edward Land's discovery.

She lives in Brittany, on the north-west
coast of France. She was only 11 when
she stumbled across a Dawn Spirit.

Chloe is now the world's leading expert on
Dawn Spirits. We at the Magical Unicorn
Society are indebted to her for her help.

A New Dawn

It was early morning – Chloe's favourite time to be on the beach. A family of seals basked on the empty sand, puffins perched on the lighthouse at the end of the rocky jetty and noisy gulls circled in the sky. On the horizon, the sun was just rising over the Atlantic Ocean.

Staring out at the sea, Chloe wished she could share the view with Matilde, but her oldest friend was back in Paris, where Chloe and her mum had lived until a few weeks ago. She felt a pang of loneliness. On a Saturday morning, Matilde would probably be playing in the park or buying pastries at the market.

Chloe sighed and got up, brushing sand off her shorts. Wandering down to the water's edge, she could see all sorts of bird tracks in the wet sand and even hoofprints from someone's early morning horse ride. Chloe moved towards the rock pools, her eyes peeled for shells and sea creatures.

"Hey!" a girl's voice suddenly called out from behind her. Chloe turned and saw Aurelie, a girl she'd seen at school. "Looks like we both had the same idea. Come and see what I found."

"Oh wow," Chloe said, when she'd picked her way across the slippery rocks and seen the starfish that was clinging to a barnacle-covered boulder. "That's pretty cool."

"Right?" Aurelie said. "C'mon, let's see what else we can find." The girls began combing the beach together, pointing out crabs scuttling among the pebbles and tiny fish swimming in the rock pools. To Chloe's surprise, it was easy to talk to Aurelie; it turned out they both loved animals.

"What's this?" asked Chloe, holding up a spiral-shaped shell. A clutch of legs wriggled wildly, then disappeared back inside.

"A hermit crab," said Aurelie. "They find abandoned shells and move into them when their own shell gets too small."

"Maybe they should stay put," Chloe said, putting the hermit crab back. "Moving's not all it's made out to be."

"So why did you leave Paris?" Aurelie asked.

"My mum is a vet," Chloe explained. "Dr Bernard was retiring, so Mum took over his practice here."

"Do you miss the city?" asked Aurelie.

Chloe nodded. "There's not exactly as much going on here ..."

Aurelie looked downcast. "Don't you like anything here?"

"I love the beach and all the animals," admitted Chloe, feeling a bit bad. Then she added, "And the crepes from the creperie."

"The ones with chocolate sauce are my favourite," Aurelie said, grinning. "C'mon, let's go up into the dunes. I know a good place to spot birds."

As they approached the dunes, though, Chloe heard a noise. But it wasn't the squawk of a sea gull – it sounded like a whinny. She suddenly remembered the hoofprints in the sand.

"Do you hear that?" she asked Aurelie. The girls scrambled up the sloping sand dunes, following the sound.

"Look!" cried Chloe, pointing. A faint, yellow glow was coming from the long grass.

When they got closer, Chloe gasped. There, nestled in the sand, was a pale blue horse. Its mane and tail were royal blue with pink ends, and there was a bright yellow horn on its head.

Aurelie clutched Chloe's arm. "What in the world is that?"

"I *think* it's a *unicorn!*" Chloe gasped.

The creature whinnied pitifully.

"Where on Earth has it come from?" Chloe whispered. Then, she noticed something on its leg. "It's hurt."

"Oh no!" Aurelie said, seeing the unicorn's eyes filled with pain, the gash on its leg and the blood on the sand.

"Come on," Chloe said. "My mum will know what to do."

Aurelie dropped her basket and they sprinted across the sand to Chloe's cottage by the edge of the beach. Behind the house was an old stable block and her mum's veterinary surgery.

"Mum!" shouted Chloe, bursting into the surgery. "Come quick! We've found a wounded animal."

Grabbing her medical bag, Chloe's mum followed them without asking questions. Chloe had a feeling it was going to be a surreal morning – she'd never seen anything like a unicorn in Paris.

"Oh!" exclaimed Chloe's mum, sinking to her knees as she gazed at the magical creature in the sand. "I don't recognize this type."

Chloe stared at her mother, amazed. "You mean you've seen a unicorn before?"

Her mother nodded. "I'll explain later. First, we need to help it."

The unicorn whinnied in pain.

"It must have scraped its leg against a rock," said Chloe's mum, examining the wound.

"Can you make it better?" asked Aurelie.

"Yes, but I'm going to need your help. Medicines aren't much use to unicorns. I need you both to gather seaweed for me – quick as you can."

The girls quickly ran down to the beach. They tipped out the shells Aurelie had been gathering in her basket and filled it with different varieties of seaweed: glossy green sea spaghetti, bubbly yellow bladderwrack and dark red bunches of Irish moss. Scrambling across the sharp rocks, Chloe scratched her leg, just like the unicorn. She cried out in pain but kept going, knowing she had to help the magical creature. Holding the heavy basket together, Chloe and Aurelie lugged it back up the dunes.

"Thanks," said Chloe's mum. She squeezed the seaweed into a compress and patted it gently against the unicorn's injured leg. "This will draw out any infection and reduce the swelling."

"Don't worry," Chloe whispered in the unicorn's ear. "We're going to make you better, wherever it is you've come from!"

Chloe's mum glanced up at the sky. The sun was higher now. "We need to move the unicorn before people start arriving for a day at the beach."

Chloe looked up and saw some dog walkers over the crest of the dune. Who knows what they would've made of the magical creature if they saw it. Chloe, her mum and Aurelie encouraged the unicorn to its feet and together they walked the short distance back to Chloe's house.

They led the unicorn into the stables, where it collapsed on a bed of straw and fell fast asleep.

"I need to make a call," said Chloe's mother, hurrying out of the stable.

"Is this really happening?" Aurelie asked Chloe.

Chloe looked down at the unicorn. For something that wasn't supposed to exist, it certainly looked real.

When Chloe's mum returned, she started to explain. "When I was a girl, my family went skiing and I met a Mountain Jewel unicorn. That started my love of unicorns and is part of the reason I wanted to be a vet. I've worked for the Magical Unicorn Society in secret for years, wherever and whenever they've needed me. Part of the reason we moved is because it was rumoured a new kind of unicorn had been spotted along this coastline, and now we know it's true."

Chloe and Aurelie exchanged amazed looks.

"My contact at the Society headquarters said that this unicorn is a rare Dawn Spirit. They're a brand-new type of unicorn family, and apparently their magic can grant wishes."

"Well I know what I would wish for," said Aurelie. "For it to get better! Oh, and to heal your leg, Chloe."

Chloe smiled in agreement.

"Why don't you two pick some sea campion," said Chloe's mum. "Eating it will help it get its strength back."

The girls went along the shingle and picked handfuls of the wildflower. When they returned to the stable, they fed the flowers to the unicorn. Chloe giggled as its chomping lips nuzzled her palm.

Aurelie spent the rest of the day with Chloe. They cared for the unicorn, feeding it flowers and applying fresh dressings to its leg. By the evening, the unicorn was looking much better. The wound on its leg was healing, its brilliant eyes were free of pain and its horn sparkled brightly with health. When it was time for Aurelie to go home, Chloe said goodbye to her new friend.

"Come back tomorrow before sunrise," said Chloe's mum, "and you girls can release the Dawn Spirit together."

*

The next morning, the girls led the unicorn through the garden and out to the beach, where the sun was just peeking out over the horizon. Chloe stroked its mane and silently made a wish. Golden sparkles of magic shot out of its horn and swirled around both girls. Chloe felt that her leg was instantly healed.

"Wow. That doesn't happen every day," Aurelie smiled.

"No kidding!" said Chloe, laughing, as she realized she'd made a new friend.

When she returned home, her mum said, "Guess what? I've just had an email from Matilde's mum. They're coming here for a holiday."

Chloe smiled. The Dawn Spirit had granted her wish of seeing her oldest friend. But that wasn't all the unicorn had done – it'd helped her to make a new friend, too!

UNICORNS AND YOU

Everyone has a unique personality and we're
all drawn to different types of unicorn. Discover
which family of unicorn best represents you, then
find out what that means over the next pages.

Make time to
chat to them and tell
a joke to cheer them
up. Laughter is the
best medicine.

A fun, music-filled
disco with dancing,
balloons, cake and
party games.

*One of your guests
seems upset. What
do you do?*

Pull them on to
the dancefloor and
get them moving.
Dancing makes
everything better.

START
*What would be your
dream birthday party?*

You're first to
volunteer. You love
leading everyone up
the climbing wall.

An outdoors
adventure, where you
go climbing, canoeing
and camping.

*Your group of friends
needs a team leader.
What do you do?*

You're happy for
someone else to take
the lead, as long as
everyone is having fun.

You decide to move the party outside. Where do you go?

Go for a big woodland walk, spotting pretty flowers and animals.

WOODLAND FLOWER

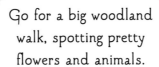

Build a bonfire on the beach and toast marshmallows.

DAWN SPIRIT

There's a big surprise finale to the party. What will it be?

A giant bouncy castle – everyone jumps and plays.

STORM CHASER

A karaoke machine – everyone sings their hearts out.

DESERT FLAME

It's time to go rafting down a river. Which do you prefer?

Solo-kayaking. It's best to be in control.

ICE WANDERER

A big raft with your friends. It's a team effort.

MOUNTAIN JEWEL

Everyone decides to set up camp for the night. How do you help?

You pitch the tent – you're really practical.

WATER MOON

You decorate, making the tents nice and cosy.

SHADOW NIGHT

WATER MOONS

Element: Water
Traits: Helpful, clever, open-minded
Symbol: Crescent moon
Colour: Bright turquoise

SHADOW NIGHTS

Element: Air
Traits: Creative, sensitive, dreamer
Symbol: Star
Colour: Midnight black

WOODLAND FLOWERS

Element: Earth
Traits: Gentle, kind, friendly
Symbol: Rose
Colour: Mossy green

ICE WANDERERS

Element: Water
Traits: Brave, strong, independent
Symbol: Snowflake
Colour: Snowy white

STORM CHASERS

Element: Fire
Traits: Confident, forceful, dramatic
Symbol: Lightning
Colour: Electric yellow

MOUNTAIN JEWELS

Element: Earth
Traits: Loyal, strong, resilient
Symbol: Diamond
Colour: Burnt orange

DESERT FLAMES

Element: Fire
Traits: Passionate, bright, truthful
Symbol: Flame
Colour: Ruby red

DAWN SPIRITS

Element: Air
Traits: Caring, thoughtful, optimistic
Symbol: The sun
Colour: Sunrise pink

Joining the Society

Now it's up to you, reader, to continue the great work of the Magical Unicorn Society. As you have seen, anyone can have an encounter with a unicorn and it often happens when it's least expected.

Why not become a member of the Magical Unicorn Society, itself? The first step is to memorize the Society's special oath:

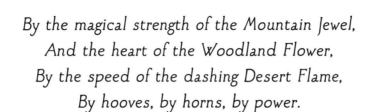

By the magical strength of the Mountain Jewel,
And the heart of the Woodland Flower,
By the speed of the dashing Desert Flame,
By hooves, by horns, by power.

I swear to hold the secret close,
To protect unicorns of every variety.
I am proud to be an enchanted member
of the Magical Unicorn Society!

Then, visit our website and follow the instructions:

www.magicalunicornsociety.co.uk
#MagicalUnicornSociety

Remember, all you have to do to find a unicorn is keep your eyes peeled and your ears alert.

Good luck, and happy unicorn spotting!